Living

ɔyal Festival Hall
the South Bank

T etry Library

al Hall   5

D1422246

To Daniel and Rebecca

Barbara Bentley

Living next to Leda

seren

seren
is the book imprint of
Poetry Wales Press Ltd.
First Floor, 2 Wyndham Street
Bridgend, Wales, CF31 1EF

13/3/97

© Barbara Bentley, 1996

Cataloguing In Publication Data for this book
is available from the British Library

ISBN: 1-85411-159-0

The publisher works with the financial assistance of the
Arts Council of Wales

Cover painting:
'Leda', 1948, by Paul Delvaux
by permission of the Tate Gallery

Printed by
Creative Print & Design Wales
Ebbw Vale

Contents

Binding Promise

My father, the proud mandarin,
promised me an emperor.

And I, a little empress of the gardens,
ran barefoot through the seasons.

Giant peony petals were scarves
drifting down to tilled mahogany.

Stiff shoots in the paddy fields
rustled my calves like brocade.

In deference to me, willows bowed.
They whispered *Empress* as I passed.

One day, the gardener took his axe
to the branches of a wilful tree.

Wings crammed the sky like omens
when the butchered boughs fell.

My mother tended, watched over me,
assessing with her gardener's eye.

When I grew too wilful, she said
the gods judged the time propitious.

She pruned my feet, then bound them.
Scarlet peonies for a connoisseur.

Wings in my throat stifled pain
mute as emperors' nightingales.

Unbolted before me, my future
was a skein of rich red silk:

my own sumptuous bandages
unravelling toward the palace.

Siren

It's just a game. A mermaid
blows her siren song
in the North Atlantic cold,
luring sailors who steer
the southern track through
bitter waters. *Ring-a-ring-a-roses*
she sings, checking for blemishes
in her compact mirror,
watching the floating palace
steaming towards her.
She garlands her hair
with a pocketful of posies,
hoping a sailor will notice her.

In sharp air, she senses
Marconi patter — three dashes,
three dots, three dashes. So,
her rhyme has charmed one.
She waits on ice, preening herself,
jollied along by the distant
sounds of the palace band —
ragtime rhythms, French songs.
Then a hymnal as the ship lists,
its constellation of lights
eclipsed in black waters.
Atichoo, Atichoo,
they all go down.

Down at the bottom, she moves
amongst dummies. Whoo. So many.
Furs and jewels cling to some.
Through cracked Versailles mirrors
they wear silly fairground faces.
Her fishtail smacks against heavy limbs
as she weaves in and out,
dodging dead men's fingers.

Before mother calls, asking
what the hell she's been doing,
she will find her sailor. She will thrust
her mouth to his. Give him the roaring sea.

Noah's Wife

i.

It was once a dip in the middle of the field.
When the heavens opened, we watched it
through the bloom on the glass. It widened
and deepened, threatening us.

But we kept to our routine, the same
as ever. Noah and the boys tinkered
in the shed, making things. They're handymen.
I tidied up. You never know who might call.

I ruined a perm taking tea to the men.
We dunked thin arrowroots in mugs
full of rainwater, while the World At One voice
said emergency services were stretched.

When the planks were tipped on our front,
I told the drivers to take them right back.
But no, Noah said, he'd ordered them.
Go inside, he said, this is man's work.

All day and night he and the boys graft,
smoothing grooves, slotting in tongues. Shavings drop
like rotting leaves. He comes in reeking of creosote,
trailing mud over my best Wilton; his eyes

turbulent as the weather. He shoves arthritic hands
under hot water. I tell him, stick to fruit bowls
and coffee tables, and things you know about.
He says I sound like a dripping tap.

ii.

They're building a warehouse
three storeys high. It juts
like a rockface into the sky.
Incy Wincy Spider can't climb
so high.
The skies are grey
and nameless. Rain names
the sky.
I know your names.
Japheth. Ham. Shem.
The three knowers, named
after him.
In the beginning
a girl scrawled her name.
But she can't recollect
her own ink swirl. Rain
smudged it out.
It's in the gutter with
a fallen spider.
They call me
Noah's wife, Mother.
I am no other.
They're building
a warehouse three storeys
high. It's a secret.
I'm not in on it.
For the life of me
I don't know why.

iii.

My lawn's pocked with hoof marks,
and the Wilton's ruined. It's enough
to make you weep. Course, the telly's finished.
All that filth. It was time they put a stop to it.
I'm up here, barricaded in.

Today, a heron landed. I keep an eye out
to catch it soar above the lake,
shredding clouds with arched, slowbeating wings
that drip rainwater.

Noah said it was up to me, but I told him
I wasn't going to drift
in a floating warehouse with all that rabble.
God knows what might happen.
Someone needs to look after the house.

The heron hasn't budged. It stays so still,
like an emblem worked in grey yarns.
It's waiting for a shimmer that might mean food,
but there's no fish in our lake.

The old fool insisted he was making history.
History, I said, what about the gutters
and that broken overflow? Don't talk to me
about history. I've borne three sons and put up
with you and your DIY for years.

It's safer here, watching watersilk patterns
stipple the walls. Each morning I blot the sodden ledge,
then wipe away mildew that thrives at the corners.
The veneer comes away like flaking bark.

I stand quite still at the window,
waiting for clouds to break.
There's a heron and the thrum of rain.
There's my name, Noah's Wife, scrawled
in condensation, and running.

Waking Beauty

Some old drunk was cursing
when the strobe lights shattered.
Amps leaned like headstones.
A splinter pierced my heart.

Then there was nothing
but a neurologist's torch.
The monitor scanned a dead straight,
so they switched me off.

But they put me on ice
as luxury goods under glass.
I was shelved and labelled.
Years hardened like frost,

till a frog prince blundered in.
From his underground home
he braved the nuclear winds
of a radioactive storm,

and he groped through stunted trees
to claim his impeccable prize.
I was won with a tainted kiss
and the bribe of a blasted rose.

With his reviving breath
he broke the charm, *Display Until.*
Ice fell like spindles
from my cryogenic cell.

This lab is our palace.
Though my prince is sick,
each night he tries for a son
and heir, a paragon.

But I have long passed
my use-by date.
The buds outside are nipped
and I yearn to sleep.

Living Next to Leda

Leda swore she could hear a swan. I ask you. A swan.
They're supposed to be mute. But she insisted
the noise came across as white sound.
Leda had a nervous tic triggered by
sparrows that twitched in her garden.
She said they flitted about like bits of grit
granted flight. When she got jittery,
she tuned into white sound, more calming
than a tranquiliser. At dusk, she strolled to the park
and watched swans nuzzling in lint-soft wings.
According to Leda, swans have poise.

Not like sparrows. Once, one bashed against Leda's pane.
There were feathers and beads unstrung on glass
like the stuff which sticks to free range eggs.
She couldn't touch it. She cringed. So I put the kettle on
and cleaned it up, while she rocked and focussed
on white sound. For weeks she was calm,
until a sparrow flew in. She had to brace herself
to cup the moth-cased heart. A choke of fluff
and the tickle of spindly legs was still on her palms,
she said, days later, on her way to the park.
Her pockets bulged with bread.

ii.

They took her in. Crazy Leda who heard swans
and sat by the lake in the dark
was found in her Hygena-white bedroom,
smothering bruises in an eiderdown quilt
and pillows stuffed with real curled feathers.

I went to visit. She asked for slices of bread
which she crammed in her locker. On bad days
she flew from room to room, chasing something.
Swansong, she said. Poor Leda. A bundle of nerves.
When she crashed into walls, they had to restrain her.

I don't breathe a word of Leda's version:
how a cygnet approached, not in fury
but as an emissary. She stroked angel wings,
and drawn by the flame that tipped the bill,
she entered the jet eye and was transformed.

Whatever happened, it was all hushed up.
She's stabilised now. Soon, there'll be twins.
I imagine her weaning two scrawny fledglings,
open-mouthed and insistent for more, more,
while the bastard that did this flies free.

Three Graces

Their brakes are on. Teas all round
for three old biddies in Woolworth's café.
Aglaia, 'the brilliant', lolls in her wheelchair,
mouth gaping, dentures clicking, three sheets
to the wind. Nymphs on the next table
suck on milkshakes, try not to stare.

Thalia, 'the one who brought flowers',
brings nothing but a Kwiksave carrier
slung over wheelchair handles. Plastic
orchids on formica unlock a word
that once came free with Daz.
'Daffs,' she says. Daft as a brush.

On her best herringbone, Euphrosyne
brings up tea. 'She who rejoices the heart'
is wiped clean; tucked in her crocheted
blanket, poor thing. There's a screw
missing. A sticker on her wheelchair
says *I love my Lamborghini.*

Nymphs chatter; light cigarettes.
Aglaia, Thalia, and Euphrosyne
passively smoke. You'd think it was dope,
the way they smile euphorically
at nothing. They clasp their attendants'
hands firmly as Freemasons.

Their carers smile. They know.
'Right, ladies. Time to go. Mind
your toes.' Their brakes are off.
The aisle's unblocked for the pretty nymphs,
Aglaia, Thalia, and Euphrosyne.

Dorcas

i.

For weeks I worked, embroidering evenings
long after the neighbours' lights went out.
Each night I untwisted crewel, teasing two strands
of silk from one skein. I locked linen between hoops,
so colours stretched to half-formed shapes.
I peered to thread an eye, then counted squares
so I knew precisely where to put the point.
Under my lamp's raw arc, fingers jabbed at holes —
in and out, in and out, right to left, then back again.
My columns packed more crosses than children's
kisses on cards. Then I straight-stitched
someone else's text till my writing hand ached
and the sticky needle wouldn't bend to my will.

ii.

Some nights, I got punch drunk, and then, I swear,
the lounge opened up to a high vaulted room.
Patio glass transformed to mullioned windows
and light filtered through like frozen breath.
The hiss of gas stopped, and in its place,
damp logs spluttered in an open grate.
In the cold glow, a figure stood at her frame,
patiently transcribing to hessian; writing
in meticulous script her copied book of hours.
She looked tired, and I should have said, leave it.
But the rhythm of her fingers charmed me.
I dozed and when I woke the room was itself
but for the woodsmoke and shavings of yarn on the rug.

iii.

I never knew her name, but call her Dorcas,
descendant of the bible woman who stitched pity
in the garments she made for widows.
My Dorcas smiles on seamstresses: those
who click at two-ply matinee coats,
or whose heels on the treadle control the stylus.
She watches over women who full-stop evenings
with a gentle tug of a French Knot; and to those
who drop stitches, she offers consolation
with her Mona Lisa smile. *HOME SWEET HOME ABC 123*
Dorcas perished long ago on threadbare cloth,
so I work at this design, deleting and inserting, shaping
on the Amstrad screen till I'm ready to print her.
I save my original, and in my name, I make her.

Double Glazed

The streaks grow larger. They're trapped between panes
so I can't get at them. I've tried, but no.
Duster and vinegar won't make them clean.

Air sneaked in through a broken seal. Its sheen
expanded, condensed as water, and so
the streaks grow larger. They're trapped between panes.

Once, I limbo'd beneath the guillotine
edge of sash to windolene a see-through glow.
Duster and vinegar won't make them clean —

those pigeon-flecked years. I shammy'd a gleam
on spattered glass till it was spotless. Now,
the streaks grow larger. They're trapped between panes

like shadows on x-rays. Light intervenes
so tumours are pressed flowers, and you know
duster and vinegar won't make them clean.

But I scrub at stubborn-as-muck stains; blow,
scour with red-raw hands at dirt that won't go.
The streaks grow larger. They're trapped between panes.
Duster and vinegar won't make them clean.

Medusa

It was easy. She stole into his house
while the wife was out.
They couldn't help themselves.
She was sure there was something in it.

Come morning, grit scratches at
the soft membrane of her eye.
She searches for the irritant.
But there's nothing in it.

Doctor beams in on the cornea.
He offers drops, assuring her
that there's nothing in it.
Whatever was in it, is gone.

But she can't open it.
Pus solders her lashes.
The kids avert their eyes
from the eye with nothing in it

but venom. She wonders why
she never saw it coming —
this foreign body, infecting
the livid folds of her lower lid.

But now she sees
there was never anything in it,
she will fix him.
He will turn to stone.

Eye Test

When he looms before her,
the pin light of his torch
pricking her pupils, she can see
his strafed skin, so cratered
because he is less than an eyelash away.
There is a glisten that could be orange zest.
She can see his nostrils, at this range
dark and filamented, and feel his breath
warming her cheek like a soft touch.

She wonders how she must seem to him —
whether her blemishes are magnified,
or whether his professional stance
has made him myopic, or blind.

So this transaction is a tacit agreement
that the two parties decline the invitation
of a lover's intimacy.

Unless she misreads his enlarged smile
and the braille of his fingers
smoothing hair behind ears
as he comes in close for the fitting.

Nervosa

When Bertie Bassett plumped my pillows,
kissed my cheek and tucked me in,
I knew I'd overdosed on
buttons, nuggets, cubes, twists,

cream rocks and liquorice chips.
I woke with E numbers in my mouth.
Coconut lodged between teeth
nagged at me, so

with two fingers, I thrust out
modified starch and gelatin,
glazing agents and flavourings.
I'm cleaned out now. I'm better.

But it's chilly. Cold as blubber,
the hot water bottle's unhuggable.
I need something to warm me,
to give comfort. Bertie's gone.

I think of mum and dad asleep,
pale and cool like two slabs
of thick white chocolate. They're
so sweet, I could eat them.

Something to Eat

The waitress pours coke. She adds ice,
lemon, parasol, maraschino cherry,
and a devil's long spoon, flattened
like a doctor's spatula. This is
a vaudeville Alka Seltzer.

We're a table number, an odd one.
The waitress makes space amongst cruets,
ash tray, family offers. When she asks
if that's all, sir, she picks up your wink
with the empty glasses.

You ponder a sliver of green
pepper. You prod it, skewer it,
and finish it off. You will not
eat meat. It is morally wrong.
You would not hurt a living thing.

Red tissues are fisted in rings. They're
bleeding hearts. I'm breaking my bread,
puncturing the cheesed crust of something
vegetarian. Is that broccoli? You brought me here.
You paid. It would end the weekend nicely,

you said. A spear sticks in my throat.
I wash it down with the real thing.
You reach for condiments in the carousel,
dipping in, then spooning out
a flavour more to your liking.

Something to be Seen Dead In

I want to be buried in
my jaunty PVC swing
back sexy mac with the fly
away collar and maxi
zip that zithers when you pull
it, and big hip pockets for
mints that goo the lining, paper
backs, a Sony Walkman, and
Motown Chartbusters Volume
One.

I want to be buried in
my unfunereal Bat
Man Wham Zap Pow black as tar
mac, shinier than a Bryl
Creem gloss; my Emma Avenge-
ing wrap with the go-faster
seams in genuine ICI
rotproof plastic, proofed against
mould and worms; my Dracula
drape to be seen dead in come
the Wilson Pickett Midnight
Hour.

I want to be buried in
a flurry of black, rooks in
the trees, lamenting. You can
send me off in your top hats
and tails, your little jet cock-
tail frocks, your patent spats and
tall stilettos; and while The
Stones pelt my lid as you drop
me down to *Paint It Black*, I'll
snuggle in my vacuum-packed
Black Magic box, with the rose
chucked on top, all because the
lady loves a lively death in
her devastatingly black
mac.

24

Head in the Clouds

As she struggled with difficult concepts
that ripened in the loft,
just the merest hint of a breeze
whispered at her shoulders.

She had her back to the sun, so she could
concentrate on the book, instead of gazing
through the velux on an open field
where cows slumped in the parched grass.

But a trickle of sound disturbed her.
A dog yapping. A neighbour pegging out
washing. Then, a distinct rippling
and splashing. So she turned and looked out,

half expecting children on the lawn,
playing with the hose. But no. There,
in the open field, where last year's
rains still gathered in the shrinking pond,

the cows were paddling. They paddled
like old men who had come to the water,
rolled up their trousers, and felt liquid
lapping at their hardened soles.

She watched as they cooled their hooves
and shifted their weight, the great
dalmatian bulks blotching the pond
to monochrome clouds.

Water gurgled as her textbooks
went under. She closed her eyes,
and amoeba swam in the ebb
of deep, bovine sounds.

Grace

For the time when there's no time
to do it all, when you're sick of
spinning saucers on poles and they're all
wobbling, falling down.

For the time when you're in bed
imagining the unironed erupting
through the ceiling, the plaster cracking
under bone-dry weight.

For the time when memoranda
nest in your pigeon hole, then
fly free before you have time
to trap them, and your black brief case
is leaden at the bottom of the bed
like a guilty conscience.

For the time when your stop-go
ongoing relationship is definitely
stop because he's too busy
and anyway, for you, the kids come first.

For the time when you set the alarm
for some no-time hour, just to catch up,
so you'll have time for the kids,
instead of snarling at them.

For 4am in the morning when
the milk's not come, the letters
still choke in the postman's bag,
the news hasn't happened yet,
the water in the kettle is
stone cold, the insomniac
switches on to night-time TV,
while the rest of us entropy
in reassuring duvets.

For that time, Lord,
give me grace.
Give me a Colgate sticker
for the bathroom mirror,
that one of the beaming man
with the orange hair and the blue eyes
and a grin like a crescent moon,
and let me remember, Lord,
always to check out my smile.

Up for Air

Count how long I stay under, you say,
ribs bellowed as you take in air,
hold your nose and bury yourself.

Toes press against enamel curves.
A film of water blurs you,
cramped in a wedge of held breath.

I'm still counting — to you, the volume faint
as light syringed through our opaque glass.
Your heart counts louder than me...

so urgently you must obey. The waters break
and you emerge head first, choking,
sheathed in your bathwater caul.

I deliver you into the rub-a-dub towel,
blotting damp screams and pethidine
with nursery rhymes; drowned songs.

Return Ticket

With that mask on your face
and a name strapped to your wrist
you could be an evacuee, wrenched
through swing doors. There's a reflex
of disturbed air, as if a train
passed through this corridor,
and you caught it. Wheels on a track
mimic your heart's iambics
until a tunnel sucks you in
and a siren drowns you out.
You stare at your face
displayed like best china
behind the glass, beyond your grasp.

I've stamped your same day return
with my consent, and I'm mouthing
a charm against accidents.
I'm counting chevronned floor tiles,
squares on that chart clipped to your bed,
and something beginning with W.
I'm playing *I Spy* and counting you in —
Wastebin? No. Walls? No. What else?
What else? Give us a clue. I'm stressing
and unstressing syllables, like that sac
above you, tracking your breath,
or a train coming in, approaching like this —
nìl-by-mòuth nìl-by-mòuth nìl-by-mòuth.

Tidings

Sky and field are papier mâché
soaked in November rains
that hardened to this frost.
Pulped news is crusted on the grass —
Pharisees and prophets; a child in flames.

You two at the edge of the field
might be lambs. But you resolve
into my son, my daughter,
trampling over stale headlines,
shouting your own glad tidings.

At the back door, you deposit gifts:
red holly of your cheeks,
blood of headless turkeys,
farmyard stubble thorning your clothes,
frankincense loam on your boots.

Zanussi, Kenwood, Belling, Sony,
perform their minor miracles.
Bread spits under blades; chestnuts
soften on the halogen. I fling jeans
in a mixed cycle. The microwave pings.

Night gathers. There are no stars,
just lights on the tree winking back at us.
The burnt child peers through snow
stencilled on the pane. I close the curtains,
watch you yawn, then let our Christmas in.

Telephone Sonnets

i. Lines Open

A tightly stretched parchment disc, iron strip
and electromagnet, linked by wire coil
to a replicated parchment disc, iron strip
and electromagnet. Alexander Bell
toys with sound. An upset battery leaks
acid, searing his clothes. Bell's impromptu
response, vibrating on the drumskinned disc,
travels. *Watson. Please come here. I want you.*

Come here. I want you. Hardly *Eureka.*
But Watson is summoned through walls. The phone
is born. The village goes global. Speakers
rule. We encode, decode; wait for the tone.

Bell's deaf mutes are walled out of our Babel.
Come here... want you, they sign. Blindly, we babble.

ii. Voice Link

Lady, thirty, telephone literate,
(extension, answerphone, mobile and fax,
modem, and so on), with commensurate
voice skills (to conference, tease, or relax),
seeks male, sim, NS, for TLC.
Must have GSOH for pillow talk
in British or Orange or Mercury.
Voice link number 6996. Out. SWALK.

Male, desperately seeking soul fusion
WTLC, though S, tried your VL.
Wow. I'm hooked. Quell my infatuation.
Call up and hear me some time. No hard sell.

M and F souls in vocal harmony
unite in fibre optic ecstasy.

iii. Engaged

Our voices meet in a metroplex system.
Messages queue on a crowded line
as I initiate the transaction.
Hi there. I'm casual. It's his move, then mine.

We shift words like pawns. I sacrifice jokes
to cover my queen. My heart's well-hidden.
But his moves are traps. I know when he speaks
I'm tempted to use the word that's forbidden.

Stalemate. I'm hooked on his telephone voice
till the chit chat ends and the line goes dead
and the drone in my ear gives me no peace.
I have left unsaid what might have been said,

since the L *word* encoded on that line
is punched out in digits. The voice isn't mine.

iv. Fax

The faxed post slithers through a desktop chink.
FAO The Manager from his wife.
You bastard, it reads. Did you really think
I'd swallow that guff on the phone last night?
Tied up, you said. Too bloody right. Tied up
at some meeting in an en suite, no doubt —
all expenses paid while you're shacked up
with your Personal Assistant. I want out.

The kids send their love. They're strapped in the car.
I should be going. But I'm hanging on
for a phoned through telegram. If you care,
fax us. Fax, damn you. Or we're leaving home.

The document's in a tray marked *Urgent,*
FAO the boss, who's out with a client.

v. Help Line

He knows they're out there, the needy. He's seen
that kid begging for her baby. A fix,
more likely. And a tramp, in a voice thin
as meths, pleading for fags, drowned in a flux
of shoppers. Oh yes, they're out there. He needs
them. He waits by the phone for a crisis:
his voice will be oil and wine in the wounds
of some poor bugger sobbing in his office.

But victims snub him for codes they copy
in musty urinals — *RAPE, AIDS, RELATE.*
They scream down specialist lines for pity
while his phone sulks under anglepoised light,
not needed. Panadol blurs his focus.
Something rings. But his mouth is a rictus.

vi. Modem

There's nothing he wants out there. So he plugs
into the virtually real world. First, dial
a spree. No worries about Arndale thugs,
sweat, crowds, cash. Technocrats consume in style.

Next, a romp through Internet. He collects
E Mail. Sometimes the PC registers
a sudden burst of text as he connects
and responds to Cyberpunks and surfers.

Often, he strays down slip roads to Kinknet
or Throbnet. The mouse controls perversion.
His fantasies booted up on the set
are shared in a Multi-User dungeon.

He pities the Modem-less poor who own
real boredom: beer, the box, a basic phone.

vii. Answerphone

You'd laugh if you saw me, perched by the phone,
rehearsing this message. Only you said
If ever you want me, I'm always at home.
But after three beeps, the line went dead.

I can't talk into space. It's crackling snow
like an old TV after the anthem.
My voice is a quasar. How do I know
you'll ever receive me, now you're a phantom?

Answer me, please, or I'll make you up, mum.
A lap to sit on. Long conversations
till I'd gone far enough. I'm far from home
but cable-linked. You sever connections

when you say, *Just leave your name and number,*
and I'll get back to you. Will you, I wonder?

viii. Number Withheld

I'm X directory. My private number's
a secret, like the codes I learn by heart
to guard my plastic cards from swindlers.
I've healthy accounts and I don't get hurt.

I have no callers but those I can trust.
My combination's safe from intruders.
You know the sort. Cranks. Smooth talkers who boast.
Insinuations from heavy breathers.

I kept the phone in the lounge. But I found
that like a watched kettle, it never sang.
It's in the hall now. When I'm accessed by friends
I open up slowly. The handset rings.

I speak. Above me, the alarm's red eye
reads my moving lips like a well-trained spy.

ix. Wrong Number

It came back to me as an Elvis release —
For reasons state, return to sender.
You hadn't gone away. You weren't deceased,
but predictably, *not known at number.*

I've been to your place. I *know* your address.
My last visit prompted the letter.
On Basildon Bond I boldy transgressed
the rules of polite telephone patter.

You never read my intimate lyric.
The envelope — bent, ripped, and well-fingered —
was returned in a nondescript packet,
my words plundered by a total stranger.

I won't write again. The phone teaches tact.
Our lines might cross but my text won't be tapped.

x. National

'Mum, what's the distance?' As we drove to town
she never stopped asking. 'It's there, love.' 'Where?'
'Over there. Far away.' I pointed down
the road. We drove five miles or so before
she said, 'Mum, are we in the distance now?'
I tried to explain how we don't ever
reach the distance; how we approach it; how
we never get there. But whenever
she phoned her absent dad, she proved me wrong.
He was miles away, and yet in our room —
so palpably *dad*, she would even bring
her drawings to show him over the phone.

Phones fake distance. You can't reach it. She knows
that now. Dad's gone. Between us, distance grows.

xi. International

He notes the pale trace of a swimsuit strap
on her tanned shoulder, the Nivea'd sheen
of her face on linen, and that white stripe
bangling her wrist. Cast in gold, his wife's a dream.

It can't be true. She's the picture of health,
but during this darkest holiday night
she stopped, goldfingered. Smoothed on limbs, the gilt
of replenishing oil embalms his wife.

He's only a long distance call away
from his family. They'd interpret grief
better than foreigners. Ridged by slats, day
is a knife-pleated fan brushing his wife.

She won't stir. By phone, he must predict this,
since hours lag in Mean Time. There, she still is.

xii. Hooked

Whodunits hook you. Will the detective
arrive at the scene of the crime after
an anonymous phone call? Reflective,
will he note on Shakespeare Close, a neighbour
peering through slats in the venetian blinds,
thrilled by the *nee-naw*, the flashing blue lights,
and the prospect of scandal over the lines?
If he notes, will he care? They're scripted sights.

Like the corpse he expects by the telephone,
white fingers curled round a cold receiver,
a bullet voiding the heart caged in bone
and the line dangling like a cliffhanger.

But this time, the wire's round the victim's throat.
The phone, a blunt instrument, purrs its threat.

xiii. Disconnected

Hold the line please. I'm disconnected. Need
a zimmer. Need the lav. No. Phone first. Hold
the line. What's my line? Lady Barnett said
telephonist. Dead right. Dead now. I told
her, I said — I plug in, link up, plug out.
I am connecting you. You have a caller.
Which service do you require? In and out
day in, day out. A row of us. Tiller
girls wired to sound. Dancing hands cutting off
and linking up. The Exchange. It's all changed
now. I've no change. The matron's buggered off
with my pension. I'm broke. Broken. Hang on. Strange —
how she rings. I say *hold the line, Lady B.*
I'm disconnected. Are you receiving me?

xiv. Dead Line

At the third obliterating stroke, time
will cease, but the man with the RP voice
will still announce it, and a special team
of angels carrying cellphones will rejoice
that the time sponsored by Accurist shows
the precise moment when the Hot Line failed
and sinners in the market lost their shares
and the Gravy trains were at last derailed.

They'll chant this data. The boss will reply
by faxing judgements in prose keen as swords.
Saved souls will ascend in the toxic sky
like apostrophes freed from clinging words.

Ten seconds, twenty seconds, dot, dot, dot.
Sweet nothings fade with the speaking clock.

Home from Home

Marj drops him off at the caravan —
a static, his summer home.

He squints at sunlight, breaks the seal
of one room shuttered since last October.

'Now look after yourself, dad,
and don't forget to ring.'

He opens windows, notices the nets
rotting, the yellowed curtain wire.

He fixes the gas, turns on water,
gropes for the telly under the bed,

switches on, fiddles with the aerial,
tunes into greys, light and dark.

This is the life. Tins in the cupboard.
Pension book safe in his pocket,

a chippy down the road, a launderette.
He can rinse underpants in the sink,

hang them from his window. On the ledge above,
his family crowds round last year's calendar.

Once, he walked miles along the river,
sat on the bench by the swaying reeds,

watched dusk drain into sandflats
where waders landed, dabbled, took off.

Now, his feet drag like slurred words.
He misses the point. He just can't get to it.

Still, as long as he can draw out
at the Post Office. He can get by.

All summer he has things to do.
Cricket. Blue Peter. The Six O'Clock News.

Worn Out

This man's balanced on joists.
With calloused hands he hammers
spar to purlin. His torn vest flaps.
His shoulder blades burn.
Below, the radio blares; brickies joke
and slap the mortar. A navvy whistles;
the mixer grinds. Familiar sounds
are scaffolding. There's nothing else
between this man and the bulldozed earth.
One glance from a driver's mirror,
one gull's swoop, or a drill's shock judder,
and he could plummet down

through the decades, so that when his wife
finds his slippers shoved under the bed,
she notes his lop-sided walk sculpted
in gaping leather. One heel's perfect,
but the other's worn to the sole.
The cracked grain is a braille
she interprets. She sees the lad
who fell from rafters. She smells
his graft, his sweat, his five o'clock ache.
Now that she has him, she can bin
the slippers, those old man's shoes
stamped with a pensioner's limp.

Stroke

It's a gentle touch, so at that critical moment
life is less enticing than a Monday morning clock.

Not this. A thug bashed you against the ropes.
At the last count you got up, still ticking.

Ticking now. That click in your throat.
You cannot name those peas which you shell.
Those peas which you shell, willing
that rhythm of fingers you use for shelling.
But the fingers are shocked into stillness,
the peas so arthritic they will not yield in your hands.

To stroke your flecked hands back to stillness.
To hear your breath come as rasps, then soften

as your head nods. A clock stops as quietly
as dusk flapping at the gingham.

Moons

i. Ring

She considers gems
displayed on dark plush,
but prefers the white band
of a crescent moon

That one, she says.

With outstretched hand
he takes platinum,
leaving a slit
where the ring was set

For you, anything.

He offers the moon.
Earth darkens.
In the heavens,
stars wink.

ii. Crib

There's a moon and star
above the cot,
swinging beyond
the baby's grasp.

Mother taps a cusp
so the crescent nods.
But the thread snaps
and the planet falls.

While the baby cries
at the damage done,
mother bends to retrieve
a fallen moon.

Hush little baby,
mother sings.
Don't fret. It'll mend.
For you, anything.

iii. Garden

At night, curtains open, lights on,
the lounge projects through glass.
There's a three piece suite
on the carpeted lawn. The woman
sits on her sofa, gazing in.

The room in the garden is washed in light.
Manchester leaks through trees,
and flexed to thin air, the lounge bulb
shines. Higher still, the half moon
is a charming pendant.

Even the rowan rises like a standard lamp.
She will switch it on, so the framed prints
behind her are brought into being.
They're suspended on black, unmoved
by a wind which ruffles branches.

She could place her coffee cup
in the nesting box, then hang
her housecoat on the coppered cherry.
She could remove slippers,
feeling damp seep through the underlay,

or she could return the garden
to the moon, which will shine next week
through a Habitat paper globe.
She could erase herself simply by switching off
lights, ending with the magic lamp.

iv. Aubade

You could hear a pin drop in this room.
No pin drops. But in the shower
moisture pearls the nozzle and drips
as loudly as a pin might.

His face is moonwashed.
You stretch beyond him, to the table
where the clock has stopped; where
earrings were carelessly dropped,

and where two tumblers, heavy with
Chablis and Perrier, stand like
perspex paperweights. Hands trembling,
you sip the bland springwater.

Pearls moisten your lips.
You are parched. Your head
is a glass of dry white,
and your neck, a stem that might break.

You sink back in the pillows,
adrift as light intensifies
through drapes the colour of mulled wine.
The sensible morning dawns,

and time has run out. The shower well
is a pool of hours. Into it,
you could drop one pearl earring,
watch it glisten, and make a wish.

v. Girl

In the darkened room, I almost trip
over discarded clothes — lurex tights,
flirty skirt, flimsy shirt.
You're only nine. But I've seen you
watching yourself in the mirror,
swaying to rap, practising gestures,
rehearsing a heartbreaker twirl.

Now you sleep, calm as a lullaby.
The curtains are drawn, but
there are stars in your room —
pop singers pinned on walls.
I search your face for the child I know,
but find the woman to be in you.
You draw a tide of surprise.

Those cheekbone shadows; the plumpness
waned. Your full lips (that's
your dad) are parted, not quite
a cherub's pout; your long lashes,
dark as mascara. Goodnight.
Godbless. Here's a kiss. Your eyelids
flicker as your films unreel.

Sweet dreams. The gibbous moon
is halfway through the month,
but you're not yet tethered to
recurrence. You're free to rave
in strobe-lit fields with sheep and cattle.
Hey diddle diddle, marvel at one silly cow
who clears the predictable moon.

vi. Film Reel

Glint in his eye. Wolf glint. A skin full of drink.
Beer on his breath, stale animal breath. Sounds
from his mouth, a stream of filth. Beware,
beware, the drunkard my child.
He lurches down back streets where tenements
lean like trees. He spits at husks crinkled
in the gutter. Pints of best bitter
muzzle his language, so he moans,
curses, swears, drops to all fours, till
the moon licks clean his stinking pelt.

Smile on his face. Wolf snarl. A smile full of teeth,
yellowed and blunted. Sheathed in his pocket,
an incisor edge, the flick of cold steel.
Your shadow's in his eye; your smell's in
his nostrils... he's coming to get you, get you.
Run, run, as fast as your little legs
can carry you, past the pubs, parked cars,
ginnels of darkness which gobble you up.
Run all the way home. Bolt the door. Lock him out —
that howling thing chained to the moon.

vii. Lunacy

The moon plays hide-and-seek.
Now you see me; now you don't.
It shuttles back and forth,
a diabolo spinning across
the windscreen — over the tax disc,
then back to the right. The wiper
won't wipe that smile off its face.

Women drivers. She left the road here.
Look at those treadmarks on the verge.
From these indentations, I'd guess
fifty, sixty. There were no obstructions.
Driving conditions were clear, but
treacherous. See the frost glint.

She smiled at the decoy shimmer
through her sun roof; heard the moon
taunting *Catch me if you can.*
She closed her eyes, counted to ten,
shouted, *Coming, ready or not.*
Then foot down, spinning on marcasite,
she chased the grinning moon.

Tang

I strip the outer skin; pull off the black-eyed heads,
the feelers that stick to my fingers. Then I swallow

salt and worm. The last shrimp's gone in a gulp.
There's nothing left of this walk on the front

but an empty bag, shots of the family inside
my camera, and my palms reeking of brine.

I pinch pods and unzip them behind the shed.
I snap mint, chew a leaf, and watch out

for granddad. His panama bobs as he stoops
to unearth potatoes. He shakes them free

and checks for blight. When there's enough to scrub
and cover in salted, minted water, he stops,

teases flake and twist from his pouch,
presses it into the bowl of his pipe, lights it

and takes in his garden. Heat fizzes
on the horizon. Soon, the last of the sun

floods the spare room. At my bedside,
granddad's galleon trapped in a bottle

floats on amber. I count roses repeated
on the wall till the ship's lost in dusk.

Decades later, when I'm washing shrimp
from my hands — shrimp, which smells nothing like

the green tang of mint — that day comes back to me,
sniffed out from the rest, unearthed and freed.

A day when granddad smelt of 'baccy and soil.
As he soaped for dinner, perhaps he sieved

through dirt and got to coal-dust; inhaled
carbon as if he'd just come up from a shift.

And when our faces come back developed
everyone says how true they are.

Searching for Links

Your dad brought you back loaded with images:
a sun and a fingernail moon over the harbour,
then the milky way mapped in an unlit sky.
A shooting star. Waterfalls. Tavernas. Spiders
as big as your hands. The caves of Meganisi.

I can't get a word in. Your stories spill out
like laundry from the bursting case your dad
returns. I unzip the load and turn out pockets.
White sand. Three hundred drachma. One pebble
smoothed to bone, rippling my pool of tales

you have not heard. I dredge and find a garden
where young cocks strut and fight under dripping fuchsia.
I watch them from the porch. Gnats zither.
Bees are at the lavender. Later, half-crazed moths
bash against my paper shade. Next day

I'm wading through stunted gorse to the brink
where cliffs skelter down to sea-smoothed bones.
Somewhere there's a drowned sheep
jigsawed in the sand. I've seen the cleft jaw,
a cracked sternum, and ribs curved like combs.

Solving Nan

Nan had a stump of a thumb.
The top was lost in a cotton mill.
She varnished nine nails and boasted
that the tenth one was invisible.

Nan was mutton dressed up as lamb.
She wore tight skirts long after
her figure had gone, and ten deniers
hoisted to corsets that kept her in.

Nan wore corn pads and stilettos.
The blue threads in her calves
threatened to snap, or were roughly
tied in amateur knots.

Nan had a bosom and hot flushes.
She'd wipe her damp brow with a hanky
that was abracadabra'd
from a *Cross Your Heart* cleavage.

My souvenirs of Nan —
a bracelet, an engagement ring,
a musical teapot and
a fraying photograph...

where Nan is virgin slender, flat as
a twenties flapper. Louise Brooks eyes
woo the camera. Her hemline dusts
perfect ankles in suede T-straps.

She clutches roses and madonna lilies
that trail her crepe-de-chine gown.
The bride smiles. Captured in sepia
is the missing tip of my Nan's thumb.

Magdalene

Coal spits on the hearth.
But the guard protects.
Over its trellis flames climb,
blossoming on dark walls.

My eyes are sharp as sparks.
Towel-wrapped after hot suds
my childhood smoulders:
a happy girl, an Ovaltinie.

Into your hands, father,
you pour the clean liquid.
Methyl of surgical spirit
stings our drowsy room.

My hands shadow-play cartoons,
while yours, sculpting flesh
with oil and wasted muscle,
are slicked amber.

Sometimes my first big words
are poured from the Sloane's bottle
as milk thick with syllables —
embrocation, liniment.

Night after night
your kneading palms
work at fallen arches.
I think your touch is fire.

Airing Cupboard

Flimsy as Isadora's scarves, stockings and petticoats
are draped round pipes. On a slatted shelf,
dad's underwear crisps beneath
stiffening shirts. Each ironed crease
is sealed tight, a sharpened edge.

There's no mumness or dadness here —
no Lentheric *Tweed* or builder's sweat —
but something odourless, uncompromising
like the slub of towels hardening
at the bottom of the heap.

Bulbs pulse in dark corners. Compost dusts
the *News of the World.* On the lowest shelf, accessible,
are navy knickers, liberty bodices,
and knee socks interlocked like fists.
My name-taped blouse is starched and virtuous.

I shouldn't pry. Some things are best kept
out of harm's way. The copper tank
scalds like a reprimand as I stretch and grasp
for Dr. White's hidden box. I might be caught
red-handed, fingering his dressings.

Dr. White wears a boil-washed lab coat.
At night his voice, deep and guttural,
comes from the cabinet. Shirts and stockings
dance to his tune. They're fused at hip and sleeve
like a child's paper cut-outs, unfolding.

Beside the Sea

You're all skin and bone. Like a bare-limbed fakir
walking on nails, you struggle over shingle,
litter, and ruched sands spilling chipped shells.

I am my own parent, sitting safe on the edge,
tracking you. At the smooth, you gather speed,
scuffing sand into jet lines as you zoom

through a child's Blackpool packed in buckets
then patted out and topped with union jacks.
The donkey caravan jingles,

the flimsy windmills on broken stems
bloom like desert flowers.
But you're past all that.

Grown-ups swim in the sea.
I cannot staunch the tide where you scud stones,
paddle, go in deep.

So I wave at a flickering speck
which may or may not be you
joining the goosefleshed bathers.

Sea Life Centre, Fylde

Filthy weather. We run for cover
into rock pools, where starfish cringe
at our anemone touch. We go in deeper.
Fibre glass traps us, damming back waters
where creatures live, fathoming us.

Our hands splayed on glass are flatfish
cold on a slab. The live ones pass us by.
Eels ooze from manufactured wrecks.
We are fish-eyed. We gawk at them
through the lidless lens of *bubble domes.*

In a tidal sky, shark jag above us,
ignoring us as sea-bed trivia.
We're rendered down to marbled soaps
or dead fathers, coral-boned and pearl-eyed
unless we are thrown back to our element,

the shop. Shoals of us drift amongst gifts, then out
past cash tills to the prom, a ship's deck
lashed by storm. Waves crash at the walls.
We flounder. Rolled under my arm, the humpback
tugs, as if it could leap clean out of its poster,
hurdle tram tracks, thrash water,
and bore through the fathoms, singing.

Lines Composed on the Centenary
of Blackpool Tower

On Whit Monday 1894, in pouring rain,
the Tower was opened to visitors.

Mill-hands who'd never been beside the sea
flooded in. Five hundred excursion trains
took them to gaze at an inverted V
sign in the sky. Up the North. Brass and brains
constructed this, a colossus that strode
the town. Between its legs, a circus ring.
On top, a union jack. Crowds queued and paid
their sixpences. Small cost for everything
they'd ever dreamt of — foreign birds and fish;
Water Fairies Ballet; big cats, chimps, clowns;
Doctor Cocker's Menagerie; the posh
Pavilion Orchestra; the lift coming down
to earth. From heaven, they could see dark mills
shrinking. Cigar smoke drifted in the hills.

A hundred years on, and job seekers still
climb to heaven. No work down there. Few mills.
But inside the gold-painted tower, clowns
perform. Computers read palms. Dreams are brash
as bulbs that sequin dark nights in the town.
Bug World. Fun Zone. Jungle Jim's. Three fruits flash
on a one-armed bandit. Bingo! Winnings
clatter. Kids clap. A dove flies from the shade
of a magic hat, and somersaulting
over a five-man high column, a lad
in the ring catapults through space to strains
from the ballroom. One two three. One two three.
While partners glide, the customary rain
dances outside. Another bank holiday.

The Roller Coaster of Mirth

At the roller coaster, Walter would not
push the lever down to stop it.

Instead, he gazed at eagles
wheeling up and down the air streams.

He could make out the eyrie, built
in the girders of the Big Dipper,

and yes, an eagle swooped
and snatched a baby from its pram.

You could see the podgy arms
dangling from its cruel beak.

From the great span of wings
infantile cooing drifted

and faded, like a balloon
lost to the sky.

So Walter deserted his post.
Yes, he saw the riders going round

and round. He heard their
screaming chorus at each downturn.

But already, he was scaling
the steel web, agile as Spiderman,

breathing fast in the rarefied air.
He looked down at them, clamped

in their carriages, laughing
fit to burst. He felt giddy too,

so giddy, he let go. And as the air streams
lifted him, they split their sides laughing.

Honeymooners

When *Captain Cattle* won The Derby, Fred struck lucky.
His winnings went on Magees Best Mild and a mill girl
he met on the prom. He courted her. They waltzed
to the swelling sounds of the Wonder Wurlitzer;
watched couples promenading on Central Pier.
Candy floss was never stickier, ale never so full-bodied,
the mile never so golden as summer '22.
Gypsy Lea saw marriage in his palm.
He proposed in mid-air on the Velvet Coaster.

They came down screaming. After the wedding, Fred
                                         and Ethel
took a Seaview double. In the mills, the twenties roared.
Wakes Weeks beside the prom blew away cobwebs,
cotton dust. Black Velvets and oysters cured hangovers.
When times got tough, they danced all day for cash
and watched *The Starving Honeymoon Couple* displayed
                                               under
glass. All fake. A trick to show there's always folk
                                                   worse off
than you. They fell for it. Fred felt in his pockets
for a thre'p'ny bit. *Are we downhearted? No.*

In Rochdale vowels hard as millstone grit, Gracie urged
Sing As We Go, and they did. Their summers were medleys
crammed in an Oxo tin. Now they're past Silver,
past singing, but still together in the Seaview diner.
The lid won't shut on this year's snaps. Ethel pours
and nudges Fred. 'It's them,' she whispers,
                                       'The honeymooners' —
and hanging in the mirror, there's Fred and Ethel just as
they were, bobby dazzlers posing for the tripod camera
till bevelled glass thins them to a pair of daft beggars.

A Couple of Clowns

It takes two minutes to fluff out my eyebrows,
add a silly black tash, dickie bow, and pork pie hat.
I sling a tatty jacket over trousers hitched to braces,
so there's room for squirters, a penny whistle, custard pies.
Then I sit and wait, and watch Louis

as he pencils courtly brows that extend to his temples,
and traces perfect teardrops on a face that's primed white.
He glosses a bigger mouth over his own, pouts,
blots his new lips with petal-soft tissues,
and sets his work in a cloud of powder.
Under the ritzy bulbs he checks for cracks.
Sometimes he lets me press sequins to his cheekbones.

Louis sleeks his hair under a Pierrot hat,
then he bends and eases into slippers
that are velveteen winklepickers.
He tells me how courtiers once wore such fripperies
to lift the hems of damsels' skirts.
To hear his trumpet serenades is to know
that Louis never jests. And so, I believe him.

Later, when Louis removes his slippers,
I will cool each instep with oil of peppermint.
I will undo the collar that kissed his neck
and, my fingers slicked with the finest creme,
I will strip the porcelain from his face.

War Scarecrow

Grozny, 1995

This scarecrow has a crumpled face
screwed up in a dirty bag. There are rags
at her neck. There is dirt in her hair,
and everywhere a spattering of blood,
as if her maker had flicked the excess
from the bristles of his brush
when he had finished with her.

You'd rather remember the ramshackle man
you thought you once saw, when a train
screeched from a tunnel somewhere,
when open fields gushed at the window,
and there he was — stock-still in the corn,
beaming, cricking his neck to watch children
picking daisies beyond the hedge.

You believed in old Worzel. But he was only
the trick of the sun on a tree,
a shaft of light through a half-opened door
to the past where your grandmother played.
You can't find his smile on this girl's face.
She stares you out. She scares you.
She is there in your wildest dreams,

where she is pinned to an upright stake.
Her shoulders are nailed to a crossbar.
Her arms droop. Her head lolls.
When the war planes break cloud cover
and swoop, her voice is freed
in the scream of engines. Her burnt shape
scatters in a fall-out of cinders
as the lit field turns to rapeseed.

Skull Caps

She is having streaks. For this, she wears
a plastic cap that fits like a membrane
over her scalp, and she does not flinch
when strands of her hair are teased
through the cap's perforations, dyed,
then left to stiffen to a punk's spikes.
The excess blonde will come out
in the wash. She'll emerge sun-kissed
and the pain will be worth it.

She looks relieved when the cap comes off.
But uncle wasn't freed from the vice
that gripped his skull. He always wore
a cloche of tempered steel clamped
to his head, shielding a war wound.
I never saw it. I only saw paralysis
down his left side, and the cloth cap
he never took off. He kept the steel
plate a guarded secret, a legend.

At night, when aunt had eased him into
the big mahogany bed, then lay beside him,
she must have removed his cap and stroked
the metal that cased his brains.
Perhaps she felt for the tips of his ribs that
they'd grafted to his shattered skullbones;
wondered if she could slacken the rivets
of the hardened shell to find the kernel,
to find the man. If only she had healing hands...

Sun-streaked hair, bullets, hands that restore.
They came together in that shot of Kennedy
turning the corner, when light ricochets
off the lens, then Jackie bends over him

as he slumps, scooping something of him
from the back seat, holding him,
as if her hands could be steel, could contain
all that stuff pouring from him, still pouring
in so many playbacks, messing her chic little suit.

Lilies

Long after he'd gone
the lilies they sent
massed white

like angels hosting
above the polished rink
of her table top.

Fully opened,
their stamens probed
cleaned spaces.

They bugled judgements
to the four corners
of the silent lounge.

I can be rid of them,
she said aloud,
throwing them out —

proud Lucifers
falling to darkness
with the rest of the trash.

Later, when she drained
the yellow stink
from the vase

and scrubbed at
the ring of scum
— the dull, gold band —

she noticed her sleeve
dusted by pollen
to burnt sienna

and her fingers
stained
his chainsmoker brown.

Acknowledgements

Acknowledgements are due to the editors of the following publications where these poems first appeared, *Envoi*, *Orbis*, *Seam*, *Psychopoetica*, *PHRAS '93* and *PHRAS '96* Open Poetry Competition Winners' Anthologies, Peterloo Poets 1995 poetry poster.

Versions of 'Stroke' and 'Eye Test' appeared in *Five Women Poets* (Crocus, 1993), 'Up For Air' in *Excite the Mind* (AK Press, 1994); 'Dorcas' and 'Solving Nan' in *Poems from the Readaround: Manchester Poets* (Tarantula, 1995). 'Eye Test', 'Voice Link', 'Fax', and 'Airing Cuboard' appeared in *Burning the Bracken* (Seren, 1996).

'Something to be Seen Dead In' won first prize in the Sefton Creative Writing Competition, 1994, under a different title. 'Binding Promise' won first place in the Charterhouse International Poetry Competition, 1994, and 'Living Next to Leda' won the Wales Writers' Group Prize, Cardiff International Poetry Competition, 1994.

The author would like to thank North West Arts for the writers' bursary received for 1995-96.